THE RELUCTANT
PITCHER

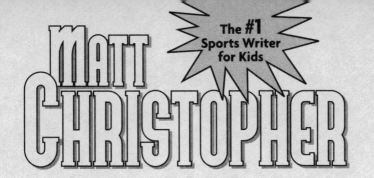

The #1
Sports Writer
for Kids

THE RELUCTANT
PITCHER

Little, Brown and Company
Boston   New York   London

for
Corky, Becky, Scotty, Jody, and Tommy

ISBN 0-316-14127-5 (pb)

Library of Congress Catalog Card Number 66-10999

10 9 8 7 6 5 4

COM-MO

Printed in the United States of America

Warm up, Wally," said Coach Hutter. "I want you to pitch the next inning."

Wally Morris had been about to sit in the dugout. He looked at Coach Hutter, a tall, wiry man with gray hair and blue eyes. Sometimes those eyes could be dark blue, especially when things didn't go right. Now they were mild blue. Wally knew that was because the Pacers were leading the Canaries by a fat margin, 8–1.

"Okay, Coach," he said.

Coach Hutter asked Pete Jason, one of

1

the substitutes, to pick up a catcher's mitt and warm up Wally. Wally took his glove off the roof of the dugout, walked with Pete behind the dugout, and started throwing.

He didn't like to pitch. He got nervous and sweaty all over when he pitched. His control was poor, too. He'd rather play right field. He didn't mind the other outfield positions, but he was getting used to right field. He liked it there. Why did the coach have to change him?

He looked over toward the batter's box and saw Ken Asher pinch-hitting for Steve Collins. It was the bottom of the fourth inning, and Wally figured that Coach Hutter was putting in substitutes.

Ken smashed out a single, and Dick Lewis came up. Why didn't the coach have Dick pitch? Dick was tall and skinny as a rail, but he had a good right arm. He had control. And he *liked* to pitch. He wore glasses because he was nearsighted, but that didn't make any difference.

Dick took a called strike, then drove a hard grounder down to short. The ball was slightly to the left of the shortstop. But he fielded it neatly and snapped it to second base. The second baseman stepped on the bag, then pegged the ball to first.

A double play!

Alan Pierce reported to the umpire, then stepped to the plate. He was batting for Terry Towns, the pitcher whose place Wally was taking.

Alan fidgeted a lot at the plate before he got ready for the pitch. He pulled at his hat, rubbed his hands up and down on the bat, jerked his shoulders, and rubbed his sneakers back and forth in the dirt. Then he swung at the first pitch, popped it high into the air, and the second baseman caught it.

Three outs.

The infielders chattered loudly and happily as Wally walked out to the mound. A buzz started up among the Pacers' fans. They were clearly surprised that Wally was going to pitch. This was the first game in which he had played any position other than the outfield.

Wally stood tall on the mound. He knew what to do on the rubber. Coach Hutter had explained it all to him over and over again.

He faced the catcher, Chris McCray, with his left foot on the rubber and his right slightly behind it. He got the signal from Chris — one finger sticking below the mitt, which meant a straight ball — then took his windup and delivered.

"Ball!"

He began to get nervous and sweaty. Chris threw the ball back to him and once more gave him the signal for a straight ball.

"Ball two!" shouted the umpire.

"Wait 'em out!" cried the Canaries' fans. "He'll walk you!"

The next pitch hit the corner for a called strike. The next two pitches were balls, and the batter got a free ticket to first.

"Stay with 'em, Wally!" yelled Coach Hutter from the dugout.

Wally put the first pitch over the plate on the next hitter. The next two throws were wide. He put the fourth pitch over, and the batter blasted it out to center field. The hit was good and solid. But J.J. Adams got under it and caught it.

The Canaries' pitcher swaggered to the plate. He was a lefty. Wally wished he would hit into a double play and get this inning over with quickly. Wally wound up and threw.

Crack! A long fly to right field! Alan

Pierce, playing in Wally's place, hustled back and caught it. A beautiful catch. The fans gave Alan a big hand.

Two outs, thought Wally. One more to go.

A little guy stepped to the plate. Wally wiped the sweat from his brow. This one should be an easy out, he thought.

Wally stepped on the rubber, stretched, and fired the ball. *Crack!* A drive over short! A real Texas leaguer! The runner on first rounded second. Left fielder Tony Wells fielded the ball quickly and pegged it in to third. The runner hustled back to second base.

Wally stared unbelievingly at the batter, who was now standing on first. A little guy, but boy, could he hit!

Coach Hutter called time and walked out to the mound.

"Relax, Wally," he said. "You're too tight.

Loosen up. Throw that ball around their knees. You can do it."

Wally nodded. He knew what he was supposed to do. He just didn't think he was any good at it. Why did Coach Hutter think so?

The coach walked off the field. Wally got ready to pitch again. There were men on first and second, and two outs. He stretched, delivered.

A hot grounder to short! It zipped past Ken Asher for a clean single.

The runner on second scored. The runner on first advanced to second, then stopped. The hitter, after running halfway to second, returned to the first-base bag.

The next hitter singled in another run. Then Wally caught a one-hopper that was hit directly at him. He threw the man out at first and walked off the field with the cheers of the Pacers' fans ringing hollowly in his ears.

What a terrible inning, he thought. Can't Coach Hutter see that I'm no pitcher? Can't he see that I play right field much better than I pitch and that I would rather play right field?

Couldn't Coach Hutter see that?

2

Chris McCray was the first man up to start the bottom of the fifth inning. Chris was stocky. Freckles sprinkled his face, and his hair was fiery red. He took a called strike, then two balls, then blasted a high pitch to deep center. It sure looked as if it were going out into the wild blue yonder. But the Canaries' outfielder sprinted back after it and made a beautiful one-handed catch.

Lee Benton grounded out, and William "Sawbones" Davis walked. Wally was up again.

He didn't feel at ease now. He was still edgy over the last half-inning.

He watched the first pitch go by. A strike.

The next looked as if it were coming close to the plate. He swung at it, then tried to hold his bat back as he saw the ball was coming in too high.

"Strike two!" said the umpire. He had swung too far.

His nerves were jumping as he waited for the next pitch. It came, low and slightly inside. He cut at it. Missed!

"Strike three!" shouted the umpire.

Wally turned and walked away from the batter's box, his head bowed. He couldn't hit when he felt edgy. And nothing made him edgier than pitching.

The Pacers trotted back out to the field.

"Just take your time out there, Wally," said Coach Hutter encouragingly as Wally picked up his glove and started for the mound. "You're better than they are."

You think so, Coach, thought Wally. But I'm not. I know I'm not.

He was glad that this was the last inning. Three outs. That was all they needed. Three outs and it would be over.

Wally walked the first batter. Chris rubbed the ball as he carried it back to the mound.

"You seem jumpy," Chris said. "What're you worried about? We're five runs ahead, and this is their last chance."

Wally took the ball from Chris. "I'm no pitcher," he said. "Why does he put me in here?"

"You're left-handed, and you have a good arm — that's why," replied Chris. "Coach Hutter knows what he's doing. Okay. Bear down, buddy and let's strike 'em out."

Chris trotted back to his position behind the plate. The shin guards and chest protector looked bulky and clumsy on him.

Wally tried to bear down on the next hitter. He threw two pitches that were just outside of the plate, then grooved the next two. But the hitter lambasted the next pitch to left center field for a neat triple, scoring a run.

Chris caught a straight-up, straight-down foul for the first out. Then J.J. nabbed a long fly to center. But the runner on third scored after tagging up, giving the Canaries two runs for the inning.

The score was 8–5 now. In two innings the Canaries had scored four runs.

Wally took off his cap and mopped his forehead with his sleeve. It was a warm day. The sun was dipping slowly toward the hills in the west. Somewhere in the distance a tractor could be heard plowing a field. From a smokestack beyond the stone quarry a mile away, a thin line of white smoke curled upward.

A great day for a ball game, thought Wally — if I could have stayed in right field.

He faced the next hitter, got the signal from Chris, stretched, and delivered one down the groove. *Crack!* A hard sizzling grounder down to third. *Get it, Rocky! Get it!* Wally pleaded silently.

Rocky ran behind the ball, fielded it nicely, and pegged it to first. Three outs.

The game was over. Wally walked off, taking in a deep breath and letting it out with relief. It was as if a weight had been removed from his shoulders.

Coach Hutter's slender, ruddy face was wreathed with a smile. He slapped Wally on the shoulder, then took his hand.

"Nice going, Wally," he said. "You're a little uncomfortable out there, but you'll come along fast. I know you will."

He looked long at Wally, his blue eyes just as mild and warm as could be.

"Do it for me, son," he said. "I'd be very happy if you would."

"Sure, Mr. Hutter," Wally promised. "If you want me to."

Wally turned and saw Sawbones Davis waiting for him. He had been given that nickname because he wanted to be a veterinarian like his father someday. He always looked as if he needed a haircut. A tooth was missing in front, and he was sticking his tongue through it.

They started walking away together and almost bumped into a man and a girl.

"Oh, excuse me," Wally said.

The man was tall and gray-haired. Wrinkles webbed the corners of his brown eyes.

"Hello, boys," he said. "I'm Cab Lacey. This is my daughter, Helen. You had a rough two innings out there, Wally."

"Sure did," answered Wally. "But I'm no pitcher. I don't know why he stuck me in there."

"You like the outfield better?"

"Yes. Right field especially."

Wally noticed Helen looking curiously at him and Sawbones. She was about his age. He remembered seeing Mr. Lacey at the first game, talking with Coach Hutter. But he hadn't seen Helen before.

"I agree with you, Wally," said Cab Lacey. "You look fine in right field. You have a strong left arm and can make a pretty accurate throw to either home or third base, which is very important. Seems funny that the coach put you in to pitch. That Lewis boy, and Towns, look good to me."

Wally nodded. "I think so, too," he said.

15

"Well . . ." Cab Lacey smiled and waved to them as they started to walk out of the park. "See you at the next game."

"So long," Wally and Sawbones said almost together.

"He sounds as if he knows his baseball," Sawbones observed. "Never saw his daughter before, though. You?"

"Nope," replied Wally. "I don't think Sharon has seen her either, or she would have said something."

Sharon was his older sister. She was an eighth grader and knew just about every girl in town. It was certainly strange that she hadn't met Mr. Lacey's daughter.

A smile curved Sawbones's mouth. He pressed the tip of his tongue through the spot where the tooth was missing, then drew it away.

"She was so quiet. Maybe she's stuck

on herself," he said "Some girls are like that."

"Maybe she is," said Wally. "She sure acted that way. And what I hate is anybody who's stuck-up."

"You and me both," said Sawbones.

3

After the game between the Warriors and the Blue Raiders on Wednesday, the Pacers took over the field for practice. The Warriors had won the game, 5–2, their first win in three games. The Pacers had trounced them last week. In Wally's opinion, the Warriors were hardly warriors at all.

Coach Hutter had Mr. McCray, Chris's father, knock flies out to the outfielders. Mr. McCray was short and chubby just like Chris. He said that he enjoyed helping out because it was good exercise.

Coach Hutter told the infielders to get

into their positions and gave them a ball to warm up with. Then he called Wally aside.

"I want you to practice pitching, Wally," he said. "Get one of those extra shin guards out of the bag and go over there near the dugout. I'll have Chris work with you. You have a good strong arm, Wally. And you're left-handed. You're very much like Del used to be. I would have made him into a great pitcher if . . . well, if that accident hadn't happened."

He blinked a little and went on quickly. "I'll make you a great pitcher, Wally, just like Del was going to be. You're nervous yet, but you'll get used to it. Okay?"

Wally stared at the ground. He remembered very well the accident the coach had mentioned. Wally had been there when it happened. It was two years ago. They were in a motorboat — Mr. Hutter; his son, Del; and Wally. There was an explosion, and the

19

boat seemed to tear all apart. The three of them landed in the rough lakewater, and the rear of the boat, where the motor had been, was burning fiercely.

Del and Wally were so badly hurt that they couldn't swim to shore. But Del was injured worse. So Mr. Hutter checked to make sure that Wally's life preserver was keeping him afloat, then quickly pulled Del in to shore. Then he came back after Wally. By the time they got in to shore, Del was unconscious.

The paramedics did everything they could for Del on the way to the hospital. Then the doctors took over. But it was no use. Del died in the hospital. Wally would never forget that day. Neither would he forget that Mr. Hutter had saved his life.

Even though everyone told him that it wouldn't have mattered if Del had been treated sooner, Wally still wondered. If Coach Hutter hadn't had to come back for him, would Del still be alive?

That same thought crossed his mind again now. He looked up at the coach and said, "Okay, Coach, I'll keep trying to pitch."

Coach Hutter called over to Chris Mc-Cray to catch for Wally. As Wally started for the canvas bag to get a shin guard to use for a plate, he spotted a man standing nearby. His jacket was unbuttoned, and his thick gray hair was blowing in the wind.

"Hi, Mr. Lacey," Wally greeted him. "You going to watch us practice?"

"For a while," said Cab Lacey with a smile. His daughter wasn't with him this time.

Cab Lacey watched while Wally practiced pitching. After a while Coach Hutter walked over to Mr. Lacey, spoke to him a bit, then handed Mr. Lacey the ball and bat. Mr. Lacey went to the plate and began hitting grounders to the infielders. Coach Hutter walked over behind Wally and watched Wally pitch.

"Follow through, Wally," he suggested. "When you let go of the ball, bring your arm around. Don't stop it short. You'll get more speed and won't tire so quickly."

Wally tried to do as the coach suggested, but his heart just wasn't in it.

The sun was beginning to set when Coach Hutter called it quits and rounded up the boys. By the sober expression on his face, Wally could tell that he had some news for them.

"I won't be here for our next game," he said. "I have to go away on business next week and will miss Monday's game and possibly Wednesday's. We'll have to get someone to coach you." He turned to Chris Mc-Cray's father. "Phil, how about you? You want to take over the job next week?"

Mr. McCray's chubby face spread into a wide smile. "I could, but I'd be a poor substitute, Luke. How about this gentleman?" He pointed at Cab Lacey.

"I'd be glad to," Mr. Lacey consented. "That is, if it's all right with the boys."

The boys said nothing at first. They just looked at him. He looked older than either Coach Hutter or Mr. McCray, but something about his eyes looked sharp and intelligent.

"I think Mr. Lacey will be all right," volunteered Wally.

"So do I," said Sawbones.

"I like the way he hit the ball down to us," said third baseman Rocky Newcome. "Real hard, just the way I like 'em."

Coach Hutter chuckled. "Fine. Okay, boys, you have your coach. There you are, Cab. Good luck!" He put out his hand, and Cab Lacey shook it.

The game on Monday was with the Huskies. The Huskies had won their first two games and seemed to be about the strongest team in the league. The Pacers had last raps. Wally had hoped that Mr. Lacey would put him in right field. He had told Mr. Lacey that that was where he liked to play. But Mr. Lacey had him warm up to pitch.

The Huskies began rolling with their first batter. He socked one of Wally's pitches in a clothesline drive over second for a two-bagger, then dashed to third on a neat single just out of first baseman Dick Lewis's reach. By the time the Pacers got them out, the Huskies had scored three runs.

In the second inning, the Huskies scored

two more. With two outs and two men on base, Cab Lacey called time and shifted Wally to right field. He took out Alan Pierce and had Terry Towns go to the mound.

Terry threw several warm-up pitches. Then the game resumed. The first batter blasted a hot grounder down to third. Rocky fielded it, then stepped on third for a force-out, and the bad inning was over.

The bottom of the second inning began with the Pacers trailing the Huskies 5–0. J.J. was up. He waited out the pitcher, then banged a three-two pitch to center field. It was caught.

Steve Collins walked. Dick Lewis hit into a double play, ending the inning.

Terry looked relaxed and calm on the mound. He wasn't as tall as either Dick Lewis or Wally, but he could throw hard. He held the Huskies hitless that inning.

The fans cheered and gave Terry a big

hand as he stepped up to the plate to lead off in the bottom of the third. He took a called strike, then blasted a pitch through short for a clean single. Chris flied out to left. Then Lee Benton came up and banged a double to left center, sending Terry around to third.

Hope swelled in Wally as he picked up his favorite bat and swung it from one shoulder to the other. Unless something tragic happened, he would get to bat. He felt a lot better now that he was playing in right field.

The fans yelled for Sawbones to hit, but he went down swinging.

Wally stepped to the plate. There were men on second and third, and two outs.

4

Strike!"

The ball brushed the outside corner of the plate.

Wally got set again. A left-hand hitter, he stood with his legs slightly apart and the bat held high over his shoulder.

In came the pitch. Knee high. Wally swung. Missed.

"Strike two!" yelled the umpire.

Wally stepped out of the box, bent over, and patted his sweaty hands in the dusty earth. Then he rubbed his hands together, took hold of the bat, and got back into the box.

The next pitch was a ball.

And then a pitch came in even with his knees and toward the outside corner of the plate. Wally swung.

Crack! A hard-hit grounder past the pitcher! The ball bounced out to center field for a clean single. Terry scored. A moment later Lee scored. The throw-in was to second base, holding Wally up at first.

The crowd cheered. Wally stood with both feet on the bag, his hands on his hips. He felt like smiling, but he didn't. He had done what he had wanted to do. He had knocked in two runners.

Rocky Newcome popped up to the catcher, ending the half-inning. But the scoreboard looked better now: 5–2 in favor of the Huskies.

In the top of the fourth, a ground ball was hit past Dick Lewis for a double. The next

Huskies' batter blasted a pitch to deep right center. Wally and J.J. both ran hard after it. Wally got it, saw that the first runner was heading for home, and pegged the ball in.

The ball didn't reach Chris in time, and the runner scored. The hitter rounded second and made it safely to third on the throw-in.

"No, Wally!" Cab Lacey jumped out of the dugout and shouted. "Not home! Third! Third was the play!"

Wally's throat ached. Third? Why? He had to try to stop the Huskies from getting that run, hadn't he?

Then he knew that Mr. Lacey was right. He had a good arm, but he could not possibly have gotten the runner going home. He should have thrown to third to keep the second runner from getting into an easy scoring position.

The next Huskies' batter knocked a fly out

to left field. The runner tagged up and made it to home safely, proving exactly what Cab Lacey had had in mind.

"Do you see what happened there, Wally?" Mr. Lacey said, as the half-inning ended. "If you had thrown the ball to third, you would have held the runner on second, because it was impossible to get that first runner out at home. If the man was on second, he would not have dared to take third on the fly. The throw would be too short for him to make it, and they would not have scored that last run."

"I see now," admitted Wally.

The Pacers managed to pick up two runs in the fifth. In the sixth, neither team scored. The game went to the Huskies, 7–4.

"Practice your throw-ins from right field, Wally," suggested Cab Lacey afterwards. "Just think ahead what to do with the ball if it comes to you. A good rule to follow is to throw ahead of the runner, not behind him. And throw overhand, not sidearm. Your ball won't curve as much, and your throws will be more accurate."

"I'll remember," Wally promised.

The next morning, Sawbones and Chris came over with their gloves. Wally got his glove and a bat and started out of the house through the back door.

Sharon was in the yard doing acrobatics. She was wearing a red T-shirt, white shorts, and sneakers, and was spinning through the air frontwards and then backwards.

"Look at that crazy sister of yours," said Sawbones, shaking his head. "I wouldn't do that for a million bucks."

"You *couldn't* do that for a *billion* bucks," replied Chris.

They started toward the gate. All three of them stopped almost at the same time.

A girl was standing on the sidewalk, watching Sharon with fascination.

"Look," whispered Wally. "There's Helen Lacey."

5

Helen glanced at the boys. Her face flushed. She turned and quickly started to walk down the street. Half of the time the heels of her shoes scraped against the sidewalk.

"Who does she think she is?" Sawbones muttered disgustedly. "Won't even speak."

"Maybe she's shy," said Wally.

"Shy, nothing," replied Sawbones, starting toward the gate. "Come on, let's follow her. She's going the same direction we're going, anyway."

Wally and Chris were close on Sawbones's heels as he opened the gate and hurried out.

"Who is she?" asked Chris as the three of them tried to keep up with the girl. She was walking swiftly, her blond hair bobbing on her head and her heels scraping the sidewalk more than ever.

"Cab Lacey's daughter," answered Wally. "Guess she's either shy or stuck-up."

"She's stuck-up, that's what she is," said Sawbones. "She probably thinks she's so pretty."

"I don't think she's so pretty," said Chris.

"Hey, Lacey!" yelled Sawbones. "What are you so stuck-up about?"

"Oh, cut it out, Sawbones," said Wally. "If she wants to be stuck-up, that's her business. She might never speak to us now."

Helen turned right at the end of the block and started to cross the street. There were no streetlights, just a stop sign. The town had only one main street and this was it. All out-of-town traffic flowed through here.

34

Helen glanced quickly to the left and right before stepping off the curb. Then she looked straight ahead.

A moment later, Wally heard a truck rev its motor. Out of the corner of his eye, he saw the vehicle pull away from the curb. It was moving fast as it passed the boys and headed toward the intersection.

Just then, Helen stumbled. One of her shoes fell off. Wally expected her to pick it up and finish crossing the street. But she didn't. To his horror, she stooped down and started wiggling her foot back into her shoe!

"Hey, get out of the way! There's a truck coming!" Wally cried.

"You nut, get back!" shouted Sawbones.

But she didn't move from her hunched-over position in the middle of the road.

Wally didn't wait another second. He dashed into the street and hauled Helen to her feet just as the air brakes of the truck screeched. The truck came to a full stop a mere three feet from where they were standing.

Helen stared open-mouthed, first at the truck, then at Wally. Wally grabbed her shoe and tugged her gently to the other side of the street. Once the truck had passed, Sawbones and Chris hurried over.

"What are you, crazy?" Sawbones yelled at the girl. "How come you stopped in the middle of the street like that?"

She didn't say anything. She just sat abruptly on the edge of the curb. Even though her back was to them, Wally could see that she was still frightened.

"Hey, it's okay," he said. She didn't move. The boys looked at one another. Wally shrugged and held out her shoe. "Come on, put this on and you'll be fine."

She still didn't react. Suddenly Wally had a thought. He crouched down beside her and touched her lightly on the arm. She started, then swiveled her head to look at him.

"Here's your shoe," Wally said slowly. She stared intently at his mouth as he spoke, then held her hand out for her shoe. He handed it over, and she smiled gratefully.

Sawbones shook his head. "She can't even say thank you," he said disgustedly. "How stuck-up can you get?"

She didn't turn to look at him. Not right away. Not until Wally glanced up at him. Then she looked.

And at that moment, Wally understood. He knew why she hadn't heard the truck or their warning calls.

"You — you can't hear, can you?" Wally asked carefully.

Helen was looking at his lips again. And then she shook her head no.

6

Wally, Chris, and Sawbones began practicing at the baseball field. Sawbones knocked out flies to Wally. Wally pegged them back in to him, trying hard to make the ball strike the ground in front of Chris so that Chris could catch the first bounce.

A little while later, a couple other guys showed up. Wally asked one of them to get on second, the other on third. He practiced throwing to them. When he saw his throws curving to the left, he remembered Cab Lacey's suggestion to throw overhand instead of sidearm.

He tried it a few times and found that his throws were more accurate, especially when throwing to second and pegging the real long ones to third.

Cab Lacey sure knew what he was talking about. Remembering that conversation made Wally think about Cab Lacey's daughter.

She wasn't stuck-up at all. Sawbones had been wrong.

Sawbones had apparently been thinking the same thing. When the boys took a break, he said he was feeling bad about the terrible things he'd yelled at Helen. "I wish I could swallow my own tongue sometimes," he moaned.

Wally laughed. "Look on the bright side. Maybe something awful will happen to you as punishment for your evil ways!" he said jokingly.

"I wish!" Sawbones replied.

Most of the boys got tired after two hours

and quit. Sawbones wanted to keep on practicing. But Sawbones . . . he'd practice all day long if he had someone to practice with. He'd never quit.

On Wednesday the Pacers played the Fireballs. Pitching for the Fireballs was Kim Shields, who was the best pitcher in the entire league. He was chalking up more strikeouts than any other pitcher.

Luke Hutter wasn't back yet from his Chicago trip, so Cab Lacey coached the Pacers again. Wally was glad when he saw Dick Lewis warming up with Chris. That meant that Dick would be pitching and Wally would be in the outfield.

The Fireballs had first raps. Dick mowed them down — one, two, three. Lee, leading off for the Pacers, flied out. Then Sawbones went down swinging for Kim Shields's first strikeout.

Wally, batting third, watched Kim's first two pitches carefully. He took a 1 and 1 count. Kim was a tall right-hander who looked older than he was. He had a sidearm delivery that frightened a lot of batters because the ball shot toward the plate. The batter often thought the ball was coming directly at him. He would step back and *zip!* A strike.

Kim stretched and delivered. Wally watched the ball closely. It was heading for the outside corner of the plate. Wally swung. Ball met bat near the fat end and shot like a bullet down toward third. The third baseman was playing too far to his left and couldn't field the ball. Wally crossed first base for a single.

Rocky Newcome socked a long drive to center, but it was caught for the third out.

The Fireballs took the lead in the second inning by scoring a run. In the third inning they fattened their margin by putting across two more.

Leading 3–0, the Fireballs began acting very confident. They strutted out to the field like bantam roosters in their white uniforms with red trim and red caps. So far Kim Shields had netted five strikeouts. The Pacers had only three hits, and two of them were singles off the bat of Wally Morris.

J.J. Adams led off in the bottom of the fourth. He leaped out of the box on Kim's first pitch to keep from getting hit, then fouled off three straight pitches. He took two balls for a count of 3 and 2, then leaned into a high pitch and sent it blasting out to deep left center.

The fans jumped to their feet as the ball headed for the fence. It sure looked as if it were going over. Instead it struck the fence about a foot from the top and bounced back. The left fielder raced after it, picked it up, and pegged it to third. By that time J.J. was safely there, a neat triple to his credit.

"Come on, boys. Let's get 'em," Cab Lacey kept saying. He was rubbing his face and his nose as he sat there in the dugout. Wally guessed what he was thinking. This was the second game Cab Lacey had coached in Luke Hutter's absence. He had lost the first one; now he was losing the second. Luke Hutter might not like that at all.

They couldn't score any more that inning. In the top of the fifth, the Fireballs really got on to Pacers pitcher Dick Lewis. With two outs, they hit two singles in a row. The third was a line drive right between Dick's legs. J.J. made a perfect peg from center to the pitcher's mound, keeping a runner from scoring.

Cab called time. He had Terry Towns warming up in the bull pen. He walked out to Dick, put his arm around his shoulders, and walked off the field with him. The way Dick lowered his head and smacked the ball into the pocket of his glove, you knew exactly how he felt. The Pacers' fans cheered him.

Terry went in and threw some warm-up pitches to Chris, then the game resumed.

The pitch sizzled in. *Sock!* A blow to right field! It was high — higher than Wally had ever seen hit to right on this field before.

Wally ran back, keeping his eye on the ball. Man, it was high.

The ball looked blurry for a moment. It was coming down. It looked so small, like a white pill.

Wally held out his glove. *Smack!* The ball struck the side of his glove — and bounded to the ground!

A shrill cry rose from the Pacers' fans. A cry of utter dismay!

"Oh, Wally!" J.J. groaned from center field.

Wally picked up the ball and pegged it as hard as he could to home. The first run scored. The second runner tried to score, too, but the throw was perfect and Chris tagged him out.

"Tough luck, Wally," said Cab Lacey as Wally ran in from the field. "That was a pretty high ball."

"Let's get those runs back," said Rocky Newcome. "That Kim isn't so hot."

Lee started it off with a single. Sawbones flied out. Wally kept it going with a double, his third hit of the game, scoring Lee. Rocky singled, scoring Wally, but that was as far as they went. J.J. popped out to the pitcher, and Pete Jason, pinch-hitting for Steve Collins, struck out.

The Fireballs couldn't do a thing in the top of the sixth. But neither could the Pacers when they came to bat. The game went to the Fireballs, 4–3.

7

The Pacers were at the field again on Saturday morning. Cab Lacey was there, and so was Luke Hutter. Mr. Hutter had flown back from his business trip the day before.

From the expression on Luke Hutter's face, Wally knew that something was bothering him. But Coach Hutter didn't say anything. Not until Cab Lacey mentioned it to him first.

The men were standing in a corner of the dugout. Most of the team had taken their positions in the field. Wally had stopped to tie his shoe outside the dugout. He hadn't meant to eavesdrop, but then he heard his name.

"Guess Wally Morris's faith in my coaching didn't bear out," Cab said. "We lost both games."

Luke Hutter, ready with a bat and ball to start hitting grounders to the infielders, cleared his throat.

"I don't mind that too much, Cab," he said. "That could happen even with me coaching. But why did you put him in right field?"

"That's the position he can play best," Mr. Lacey answered.

"Because Wally said so? He's a bashful boy, Cab. He just *thinks* he can play right better than he can pitch. But that boy can throw. He has the physique of a pitcher. And he's left-handed. He has everything a kid needs to be a great pitcher when he gets older."

47

"Tall left-handers make good outfielders, too, Luke," replied Mr. Lacey. "There's nothing wrong in letting Wally play right field. With that arm of his, he can throw a man out at third and at home. And he hits better when he's in the outfield because he's more confident in that position. He got three for three against the Fireballs."

"Yes. And he missed a fly ball that gave the game to them, too," Luke Hutter answered quickly.

"He made a good try," said Mr. Lacey. "That ball was real high."

"Cab," Luke said, "let's not stand here and argue about it like a couple of old fools. I've had a lot of baseball experience. I can tell who could make it as a pitcher and who could make it as an outfielder. I think that if Wally played any position other than pitcher, he'd lose out on his best opportunity in baseball."

Wally was hurt that Cab Lacey was blamed for putting him in the outfield, and embarrassed that they were talking about him. He picked up a ball and had started away when Mr. Lacey called him back.

"There you are, Wally. Say, do you know who Mr. Hutter played with? Some professional team?"

"No. He just played with a team around here, Mr. Lacey. My dad used to play with him." He squinted against the bright morning sun. "Did you ever play with a professional team, Mr. Lacey?"

"Had about five years' experience in minor league baseball, Wally," answered Cab. A warm light twinkled in his eyes. "I was with Williamsport in the New York–Pennsylvania league most of the time."

Wally stared in surprise. "Wow! What position did you play?"

"Some guy who thought he knew a lot

about baseball had tried to make a pitcher out of me. After a few years, my arm went bad and I couldn't play any other position. Without a throwing arm, you won't find a place in baseball, Wally. Well, better get going. Chris is waiting for you."

After practice all the boys began leaving the field. Luke Hutter asked Wally to wait.

"I have to tell you, Wally," Mr. Hutter said. His voice was friendly, his eyes the warmest blue Wally had ever seen them. "You really reminded me of my son, Del, out there today. I suppose that might sound foolish to you. But it isn't. You two were great pals. I had figured on both of you being on my pitching staff this year. I hope that's what you want, too."

Wally's throat was dry. He looked at Luke Hutter for a minute, then looked away. He got to thinking about the boat ride two years ago. He got to thinking about the explosion and about Mr. Hutter's pulling Del out of the water and swimming back out after him. He would have drowned if it weren't for Luke Hutter.

He met Mr. Hutter's warm blue eyes.

"Uh, sure, Coach," he said. "I mean, of course I'll pitch."

Coach Hutter clapped him on the back. "I knew it! You'll be great once you get the hang of it."

But Wally wasn't so sure. No, he wasn't sure about that at all.

8

The day the Pacers were scheduled to play the Blue Raiders was gray and dismal. It looked as if it might rain, and Wally hoped that it would. He wouldn't have to pitch then.

He was just wondering what he would do for the afternoon when the phone rang. It was Sawbones.

"Dad's going over to the dairy farm today to give all the cows their shots. He needs someone to record their ear numbers so he can be sure he got them all, and he wondered if we'd like to do it. You want to come along with us?"

"Sure," Wally replied. He wasn't as crazy about the big animals as Sawbones was, but sometimes the farmer had other animals, like dogs or goats. He checked with his mother.

"Okay," she said. "Be back by suppertime."

"Thanks, Mom." Into the telephone he said, "Okay, Sawbones. I can go. See you in a little while."

Sharon was in the backyard, practicing gymnastics. She was wearing a white T-shirt, shorts, and sneakers, and a ribbon around her head to keep her hair from falling all over her face.

It seemed as if she could twist her body any way she wanted to. She laid her hands flat against the grass and lifted her legs slowly into the air. When she had them straight up, she held herself steady for a few moments, then did a quick somersault backwards, landed on her feet, and slid her legs straight out into opposite directions — a perfect split.

She was really graceful at it. She had performed several times at the school and was sometimes asked to perform between acts of a play and at social functions.

She liked to play volleyball and Ping-Pong, too. Wally was secretly proud of her. He never told her so because she seemed to suspect it anyway.

Half an hour later, Wally and Sawbones were writing down numbers as Dr. Davis's assistant called them out. They helped out for an hour, then Dr. Davis told them they could take a break and look around for a while. "Just be sure you're back here in half an hour so we can head for home," he reminded the boys before they took off.

"Let's go to the dairy store and see if we can get a couple of chocolate milks," Sawbones suggested.

"Okay," said Wally. There was nothing he liked better than a frosty cold glass of milk. The chocolate was a bonus.

Then Wally thought about the game scheduled to start at six o'clock. He had no idea what time it was. Neither he nor Sawbones wore a wristwatch. And he couldn't tell anything from the sun, because it hadn't been out all day. It was as cloudy and sultry now as it had been hours ago.

They walked up the long driveway to the white stucco building where the dairy store was. To the right of the building was the large white house where Mr. Riker, the owner of the dairy farm, lived. Beyond the stucco building were the great red barns in which were housed the many cows that furnished the milk for the dairy.

In the summertime, the cows were permitted to graze outside in the huge fields of the farm. In the early morning hours of each day, and in the evenings, they were brought into the barns and milked with electric milking machines.

Wally and Sawbones entered through the front door. There was a large glass-door refrigerator in a corner filled with containers of milk. On a table was a small cash register. There was no one in the room.

Sawbones led the way into a large room where all the machines that filled the containers with milk were kept. The place was silent. No one was around.

"Hello!" Sawbones called.

They found a large door standing wide open.

"That's the cooler," explained Sawbones,

who walked around the place as if he had been here before. "Maybe Mr. Riker's in there."

They walked into the cooler. A pale yellow bulb was on, furnishing very little light.

"Hello?" Sawbones yelled again, a little less certain this time.

Still no answer.

Sawbones led the way around the dozens of cases of quart and half-gallon containers of milk. Wally felt the cool air gnawing through his clothes to get at his skin.

He was becoming scared. The place was dark and creepy. He didn't like it. Maybe they shouldn't have come in here. Maybe they should leave right now. It was obvious that no one was in here.

And then there was a loud *slam!* as the door shut. At the same instant the light went out, too.

Hey!"

Again and again Sawbones and Wally yelled out. But the big door didn't open.

Fright took a tighter hold of Wally. His eyes were wide open, but it was like being blind. He was in complete darkness.

And the place was silent as a graveyard.

Wally shuddered.

"Sawbones," he whispered.

"Yeah?" Sawbones croaked back.

"Let's walk straight ahead. When we come to the wall, we'll turn left and follow the wall back to the front of the cooler. We can find the door that way."

"Okay," whispered Sawbones.

Very slowly they walked through the pitch darkness straight ahead. Wally held his arms extended in front of him.

Suddenly Sawbones cried out, "Ouch!"

Wally froze. "What's the matter, Sawbones?"

"Ran into a case of milk," mumbled Sawbones sourly.

Wally heard his feet scrape across the floor.

"You okay?" he asked.

"Yeah," replied Sawbones.

Wally started to go straight ahead again. Soon his hands touched the cold, clammy wall. It sent shivers running through him.

"I've reached the wall." His voice quavered.

"Me, too," whispered Sawbones.

They walked along the wall to the left. They reached the corner, then turned left again. Seconds later Wally felt the crack where the door adjoined the casement. About the same time he heard the clang of metal and then Sawbones crying out that he had found the door handle.

The metal kept clanging.

"Well, open it!" Wally cried. "What're you waiting for?"

"I can't!" exclaimed Sawbones. "It won't open!"

He tried and tried, but the door wouldn't open. Then Wally tried. It was a strange sort of a handle, with a large knob on the end of it. He pushed it down hard, but the latch didn't budge.

His heart began to beat like a hammer. "We're locked in," he said, panic taking hold of him. "We . . . we'll freeze in here, Saw-bones!"

He looked down toward the bottom of the door. There was a faint strip of light showing underneath. He got on his knees and groped along the crack with his fingers. A narrow space was there, but not wide enough to get his fingers through.

He stood again. It was getting colder by the minute.

"What're we going to do, Sawbones?" he hissed. His heart hammered in his throat.

"I . . . I don't know!" Sawbones answered. He pounded against the door again and again. And he yelled for his dad.

But no one came to the door.

Sawbones's teeth chattered. Wally could hear them. He held his own tightly together. But he was scared. Real scared. We're freez-ing! he thought. We're freezing to death because nobody can hear us! Where is Dr. Davis? Isn't there anyone around here?

Suddenly — "Sawbones, I have an idea!" he shouted.

"What?" Sawbones asked.

"Get me a container of milk," Wally demanded. "Somebody will know that we're in here . . . sooner or later. I hope sooner."

He heard Sawbones's shoes scrape across the floor. He heard the milk being lifted from a case. A moment later Sawbones was handing it to him.

Wally took it, knelt down, and started to spill the milk through the crack underneath the door.

"Hey, that's smart, Wally," said Sawbones. "Why didn't I think of that?"

Wally grinned. "Now let's hope somebody will see the milk," he said. He spilled the whole quart of it on the floor.

Minutes passed.

All at once a terrible thought flashed through Wally's mind.

"The game's going to be starting soon, Sawbones. Maybe your dad thinks we already left to go there!"

"That's right!" cried Sawbones. Then he groaned hopelessly. "You know what this is, Wally? It's my punishment for the mean things I said about Helen Lacey!"

Wally didn't know what to say to that. Under different circumstances, it would have been funny. But Wally didn't feel like laughing just now.

10

Let's hop up and down," suggested Sawbones. "That'll keep our blood circulating and keep us from freezing."

He started hopping as soon as he mentioned it. So did Wally.

"We wouldn't freeze, anyway," Wally observed suddenly. "If the milk doesn't freeze, how can we freeze? Anyway, we can't hop all night. We'll be dead tired."

"Yeah, that's right." Sawbones sighed despairingly. Wally knew that his hopes of being rescued tonight from this dark prison were shattered.

And then there was a sound outside of the door. A voice!

The boys started hopping. They began banging upon the door with their fists.

"Open up! Open up!" yelled Sawbones.

The metal latch clicked. The door squeaked open. For a moment the light blinded the boys, but Wally could see a man standing before him. It was Mr. Riker, the owner of the dairy.

"What in the devil's name is this?" Mr. Riker cried. "Sawbones . . . Wally! How did you boys get in there?"

The air inside the machine room felt like a hot oven as the boys stepped out of the cooler. Mr. Riker shut the door behind them, and they took turns blurting out what happened. Then Wally saw a cat near his feet, lapping up the milk he had spilled through the crack underneath the door.

Mr. Riker chuckled. "It must have been

me who closed the door, Sawbones. When your dad came looking for you, I thought I'd better check back here in the store. I saw that milk on the floor and Mickey lapping it up and wondered what happened. Couldn't you open the door? It wasn't locked."

The boys stared dumbfoundedly at him. "But it was! We tried it!"

"Did you try pushing the handle *in?*" inquired Mr. Riker.

Sawbones and Wally stared at each other, looked back at Mr. Riker, and shook their heads.

"No. We just pushed it *down.*"

Mr. Riker shook his head. "That was your trouble," he said. "You have to push it *in* to open it."

He illustrated by going to the door and pushing in the handle. Sure enough, the latch opened easily.

Wally remembered the baseball game. No matter what he had thought about it before, he just had to get to that game. Even if Coach Hutter wanted him to pitch.

"What time is it, Mr. Riker?" he asked quickly.

Mr. Riker looked at his wristwatch. "Twenty after six," he answered.

"Holy smokes! Let's go, Sawbones!"

They took off with Mr. Riker staring after them. They ran down to the road and then turned toward the barn just as Dr. Davis's car pulled up next to them.

"Hey, William! Wally! Where have you two been?"

Nobody called Sawbones William except his mother and father.

"Come on, get in here!" he ordered before they had a chance to answer.

The boys piled into the car. Dr. Davis

stomped on the accelerator, and the car shot forward. The boys explained where they'd been and what had happened.

Dr. Davis laughed. "No wonder I couldn't find you! I'll take you boys home. Get into your uniforms as fast as you can, and I'll drive you to the ball field."

By the time Dr. Davis arrived at the field with the boys, the game was in the top of the fourth inning. Wally and Sawbones approached Coach Hutter nervously. He gave them a chilled look.

"Sorry we're late, Coach," Wally said. "We were locked in a cooler."

"You . . . what?"

Wally wet his lips. "We were locked in a cooler. Me and Sawbones. In Mr. Riker's milk cooler."

"That's right, Luke." Dr. Davis had come up behind the boys. He went on to explain what had happened.

Coach Hutter laughed. "That was quite an experience! Okay, Wally, you and Sawbones play some catch. I want you to pitch the next inning."

From the scoreboard in left field, Wally saw that the score was 5–2 in favor of the Blue Raiders. The Blue Raiders were batting. On the mound for the Pacers was Terry Towns.

Wally got a ball and walked to the bull pen with Sawbones. Sawbones took the team's extra catcher's mitt with him. After a few warm-up pitches, Wally began putting steam on the ball.

The Blue Raiders got out, and the Pacers came to bat. Wizard McGuire, the husky southpaw pitching for the Raiders, mowed down the Pacers with eight pitched balls and walked off the field with the Raiders' fans giving him a big hand.

Coach Hutter had Wally replace Terry on

the mound and Sawbones replace Alan
Pierce in left field. Wally worked hard to
make his pitches good. They were too good.
The Blue Raiders knocked out two singles
and scored a run before the Pacers could
stop them.

Coach Hutter tried to bolster Wally's
confidence just before he went back up on
the mound in the top of the sixth inning.
It didn't do any good. The Blue Raiders
knocked across another run. The Pacers
failed to score during their turn at bat, and
the game went to the Raiders, 7–2.

Coach Hutter was really disgusted. You
could tell that by the dark look on his face
and the dark blue of his eyes. Wally wasn't
quite certain whether the coach was disgusted because they had lost the game or
because he hadn't pitched a strong game.
Wally hoped it was because they had lost.

Wally and Sawbones looked around for Dr. Davis, expecting to ride home with him. But he wasn't there.

Cab Lacey told the boys that Dr. Davis had left just before the game had ended. He had to attend a meeting of the Board of Education, of which he was a member, so Mr. Lacey had offered to give Sawbones and Wally a ride home.

They got out of the car in front of Wally's house. Sawbones thanked Mr. Lacey and started to walk the rest of the way home. He lived only five houses away from Wally.

As Mr. Lacey began to drive away, a voice shouted from the backyard of Wally's house. "Cab!"

Mr. Lacey stopped the car. Wally saw that it was a woman. A stranger. She was sitting on one of the lawn chairs.

He walked through the gate and saw

Sharon doing her tumbling act. That sister of his. Boy! She wasn't shy to perform for *any*one.

And then he saw another girl twirl through the air in a backward somersault, then do a cartwheel — doing practically the same things Sharon was doing. She was wearing a red leotard and red tights. She was — at least, she looked like — a stranger, too.

Suddenly she stopped spinning, landed on her feet, turned to him, and smiled. She didn't say a thing to him, because she couldn't.

She was Cab Lacey's daughter.

11

Wally, this is Mrs. Lacey," Wally's mom said. "And this is her daughter, Helen."

"Hello, Mrs. Lacey," Wally said. Then he flushed a little as he looked at Helen.

"You've met her before," said Mrs. Lacey, smiling. "She told me."

Wally swallowed. "Yes," he said, remembering the truck incident. He tipped his head toward the girl. "Hello, Helen."

She nodded, too, and lifted a hand in a wave.

"She's good at reading lips," said Mrs. Lacey proudly.

Wally noticed that his dad was sitting on a lawn chair, smiling. Mr. Morris wanted to know how the game turned out, and Wally told him.

"Wish I could've seen it," said Wally's dad. "But I had a hectic day and just got home."

Another girl was there, too: Jeannie Hutter, the coach's daughter. She was younger than either Sharon or Helen, but that didn't stop her from going to bigger girls' houses. She liked to make friends with everybody.

Wally's mom was sitting on a lawn chair beside his dad. "Bring out a chair for Mr. Lacey, Wally," she said. "Did you miss much of the game?"

"Four innings of it!" he shouted over his shoulder as he ran up the porch steps.

He brought out a chair for Mr. Lacey, then sat on the porch steps. The girls were performing an act again. They bent over backwards and touched the lawn with their noses, then stood on their hands with their bodies straight in the air, as motionless as if they were statues.

"Did you tell the folks why Helen is interested in acrobatics, Elaine?" Mr. Lacey asked his wife. She blushed and smiled. "No. I just said that Helen had seen Sharon practicing here on the lawn and I thought it would be nice if the two got acquainted."

"That's just like you." Cab Lacey chuckled. "My wife's too modest. She used to be a gymnast of Olympic caliber. She would have gone to the Olympic Games, too, if it hadn't been for an injury. Strange as it seems, that's how we met. I was getting my bum throwing arm looked at when they brought Elaine in on a stretcher. I think that's the last time I've ever seen her look helpless!"

The grown-ups laughed.

"I doubt Elaine would have ever done anything with gymnastics again if it hadn't been for Helen. Helen found some old movies of Elaine performing and fell in love with the sport. She begged and pleaded her mother to teach her until Elaine finally gave in." Cab Lacey shot a glance at Wally. "Seems to me most kids know deep down what they're good at. They just need a little help getting there sometimes."

"How about you, Cab?" inquired Wally's dad. "I heard that you had some sort of career in professional baseball."

Mr. Lacey smiled shyly. "Hardly enough to talk about, Paul," he said.

"Cab is a pretty modest guy, himself," said Mrs. Lacey. "He had a professional career and was very disappointed when his arm went bad while pitching. He blamed the manager for working him too much. He had to give up baseball. I tried to make him forget it, but he loves it too much." Her eyes shone happily as she looked at Wally. "That's why you see him at all your Little League games. He really wants to help kids enjoy the game as much as he does."

Wally felt Cab Lacey looking at him again. "The thing is, I never really wanted to learn to pitch. But pitching's not for everyone, is it, Wally? I always wondered what my career would have been like if I had stuck to my guns instead of letting my manager talk me into that position."

Wally stared at his toes. He wanted to tell Mr. Lacey that he had decided to speak up to Coach Hutter. But he couldn't. He just couldn't.

"Well" — Mrs. Lacey rose hastily to her feet — "we must be going. Cab must be starving. And I bet Wally is, too."

It wasn't until she mentioned it, though, that Wally realized he was really famished. "Sort of," he said, smiling.

❖   ❖   ❖

After eating a dish of scalloped potatoes and bacon that his mom warmed up for him, Wally ran over to Sawbones Davis's house. Chris McCray was there. They were in Sawbones's room, looking over the plastic models of different animals' anatomy that Sawbones had collected.

The boys all greeted each other.

"Hey, Sawbones, could you get out your encyclopedia of sports?" asked Wally. "I want to look up something in it."

Sawbones took the encyclopedia off a shelf where about thirty other books were standing. It was a huge book of about fifteen hundred pages. Wally leafed through it.

"What're you looking for?" Chris asked wonderingly.

"I want to see if I can find it first," replied Wally.

Twenty minutes later he found what he

was looking for. His heart swelled as he read the item over twice.

"There." He pointed at it. "Read that. It's about Cab Lacey. He played with Williamsport in the New York–Penn League *four* years. He had a good pitching record. But it doesn't tell everything about him," he added discouragingly. "These books never do."

Sawbones frowned. "What doesn't it tell about him?"

"That his arm went bad. That he couldn't pitch anymore. These books don't tell you *those* things about a ballplayer."

12

Wally and Sharon were eating lunch the next day when the telephone rang. Mrs. Morris went to answer it.

"Yes, this is Ann," she said. "No. She's not here."

A moment later her eyes widened and flitted around worriedly. Wally could tell that whatever she was hearing was upsetting her considerably.

"Just a moment, Elaine," she said, and cupped her hand over the mouthpiece. "Did either of you children see Helen?" she inquired. "Helen Lacey?"

Sharon shook her head. "I haven't. Not since yesterday."

"Me neither," said Wally. His brows lifted. "Why, Mom? Don't they know where she is?"

"No. She left the house about ten-thirty and was supposed to be home by twelve."

She took her hand off the mouthpiece and told Mrs. Lacey that neither Wally nor Sharon knew where Helen was. When she hung up, she still looked extremely worried.

She sat at the table and began eating with the children.

"She might've gone to Jeannie Hutter's," Sharon said suddenly. "Jeannie followed us all over creation yesterday. Just like a shadow."

"I'll call Mrs. Hutter," Mrs. Morris said. She brushed a napkin across her mouth and again went to the phone.

Wally and Sharon watched her as she

talked to Mrs. Hutter. Her eyes went wide again and started flitting around as they did before. After a while she hung up.

"Jeannie's not home. She's gone with a friend somewhere. Mrs. Hutter doesn't know who that friend is, but she thinks it's Helen."

All at once Sharon struck the tabletop with a spoon. Both Mrs. Morris and Wally jumped, startled.

"I'll bet Jeannie took Helen to the quarry!" Sharon's voice was almost a shout. "Jeannie always likes to go to the quarry!"

"Oh, no!" exclaimed Wally. "Not there! You never know when they might blast!"

Fear enveloped Wally. He couldn't eat anymore. He was going to look for those girls. That silly Jeannie Hutter. She should have more brains than to take a girl who couldn't talk or hear to a dangerous quarry.

"I'm going to look for them!" he cried, and scrambled out the door.

"I'm going with you!" cried Sharon.

"I'll drive you!" Mrs. Morris called.

They drove down the side streets to the edge of town, then down a dirt road that led to the quarry. It was a limestone quarry, used for the manufacturing of cement.

Mrs. Morris told Wally and Sharon that she was going to find a quarry manager, then disappeared into a building. Wally climbed out of the car. After a moment, Sharon followed. Without a word, they started toward the ridge of the quarry at a run.

Wally and Sharon reached the ledge and stopped. They panted from running so hard, and from being frightened about the danger that could be facing Helen and Jeannie.

Carefully they looked below and all around the huge, gray, silent quarry. In the distance, smoke was unfurling from the tall, thin column of a small factory where the stone was hauled by trucks and crushed into many different sizes and then delivered by trucks throughout the state. Here and there were huge piles of earth covered with weeds. But the girls were not in sight.

A whistle began to blow. It started off softly, then rose higher and higher until it reached a very high pitch. It held there steadily, drowning out all the other sounds one had heard before.

It was the warning signal, indicating that in two minutes there was going to be a blast.

"They aren't here," said Wally. Relief swept over him. "Let's go."

And then Sharon's face turned white. "Wally, look! Over there! It's Jeannie and Helen!"

13

Sharon, run back and get Mom! I'll go after those girls."

Sharon stared after her brother, as if not knowing whether to obey him or go with him.

"I can get down these rocks faster than you!" Wally shouted at her. "Get going!"

She turned and scampered up the dirt road. Wally started down the side of the quarry, sliding, stumbling, hopping from one jagged rock to another. The quarry wasn't very deep. It was only seconds before he reached the bottom.

"Here!" he shouted to the girls. "Here!"

He was sure, though, that they — that Jeannie — couldn't hear him with that whistle shrieking so loudly.

He ran, stumbling again now and then, over the rough stretch of rock. There was danger in running: the chance of falling, of bruises, of spraining an ankle. Wally thought of these things, but he had to keep running. He had to get to those girls.

He saw them again. Jeannie was in front, running fast, and holding on to Helen's hand. For just an instant a tender warmth clasped Wally's heart. Jeannie was frightened for Helen. She was doing her best to help Helen out of the danger zone by hanging tightly on to her hand.

The girls saw him, too. They ran toward him.

"This is the noon hour!" cried Jeannie, as

they met. Her eyes were rimmed with tears. "I didn't know they blasted during the noon hour!"

"They blast any time of the day!" Wally yelled back. "Come on! Let's get under a ledge."

Jeannie did as Wally suggested. Wally led them swiftly back over the rocks toward the ledge. The whistle was still blowing. It must have been blowing nearly two minutes by now, he thought. At any second it would stop. There would be a pause for thirty seconds. And then the blast.

Suddenly the whistle ceased blowing. It left a silence that was almost as eerie as the piercing sound of the whistle had been.

"We have thirty seconds!" shouted Wally frantically. "Come on!"

He led them to a ledge where the wall was almost vertical. He told Jeannie to get against the wall, and gestured to Helen to do likewise. Then he stood against the wall beside them — and waited.

A moment later an explosion seemed to rock the earth beneath their feet. Far to their right side a cloud of dust burst skyward, accompanied by rocks that flew like meteors in every direction, landing in the quarry and on the empty field beside it.

Dozens of rocks came flying in the direction of Wally and the girls. None of them landed close. In a little while all the rocks had fallen. All that remained of the blast was the huge dust cloud in the distance being blown slowly away by the breeze.

Wally looked at Helen with relief and smiled. Her eyes were wide, filled with fear, astonishment. She must have felt the vibration, Wally thought. And she could see the cloud of dust. She just hadn't heard the warning whistle, and the loud noise of the blast.

The fear and astonishment disappeared quickly as she saw the smile on Wally's face. She lifted a hand and moved her fingers, and Wally figured that she was thanking him.

Another whistle blew for a few seconds, the signal that the blasting was over.

"Thank you so much, Wally," Mrs. Hutter said after he had explained the whole story. "If those girls had gotten caught in that quarry with those big rocks falling all around them, they would never have gotten out alive." She was breathing hard and perspiring freely, and Wally knew she must have been very upset by his story.

"Don't you ever go to the quarry again," she said to Jeannie, her eyes sparkling with anger. "Not ever."

Jeannie's eyes blinked with tears. "I just wanted Helen and me to be friends, Mother," she murmured sorrowfully. "She'd never seen a quarry before."

"How do you know she hasn't?"

"I asked her. I wrote the question on a piece of paper. And she answered me. She said no she hadn't, and she'd like to see it. I didn't know they blasted during the noon hour."

Mrs. Hutter's lips quivered. Slowly the anger left her eyes. She put a comforting arm around her daughter's shoulder.

"All right, Jeannie. Let's forget it now. I'll call Mrs. Lacey. I'll tell her that Helen is on her way home."

14

That evening Wally received a phone call from Mr. Hutter.

"Wally, Mrs. Hutter told me what you did today. That was a fine showing of courage."

Wally shrugged, forgetting that Mr. Hutter couldn't see him. "It wasn't much, Coach. Probably none of the stones would have hit them anyway."

"They might have if you hadn't shown up. You risked your life to save those girls." Mr. Hutter chuckled. "Jeannie thinks you're a real hero!"

Wally laughed. "Oh, I'm no hero. And

don't be mad at her, Mr. Hutter. She just didn't know that they dynamited during the noon hour."

"I know, Wally. I heard all about it. Well, good night, fella. See you at the ball park."

"Good night, Coach."

After Wally replaced the telephone receiver, he began to think a bit. If he had saved Jeannie's life, as Mr. Hutter had said he had, then he had paid back a debt he owed to Mr. Hutter for having saved his own life. He didn't have to feel that he owed a thing to Mr. Hutter anymore.

But it wasn't right to think that way either, he decided. No, the only way he was ever going to get off the mound and back into right field where he belonged was to talk to the coach directly. Cab Lacey's story had convinced him of that. He was determined to speak to the coach before the next game.

❖   ❖   ❖

But Tuesday, when the Pacers played the Warriors, Coach Hutter was too busy getting ready for the game for Wally to take him aside. Before he knew what was happening, he was on the mound again.

The Warriors had first raps. The first hitter for them was a peewee. Wally tried to throw the ball over the plate between the little guy's shoulders and knees, but just couldn't make it. The peewee walked.

The next Warrior laid down a bunt. Wally expected it. But the ball rolled toward third just inside the baseline and he couldn't get it in time. The batter was credited with a hit, and the runner on first made it safely to second.

Wally began to sweat. The fans were trying to encourage him. The infielders were trying to encourage him. But none of it did him any good. His heart pounded as he stepped to the mound. He got the signal from Chris, stretched, and delivered.

Another bunt! This time it was a poor one. The ball rolled straight toward the pitcher's mound. Wally ran forward, fielded it, and pegged to third. Rocky caught the ball for the force-out, then heaved it to second. The runner reached there in time.

The next hitter walloped a drive over second for a clean hit. A run scored. A ground ball to Rocky resulted in another out at third. Then a foul fly, which Chris caught, ended the top of the first inning.

Lee Benton started things off with a walk. Sawbones popped out to third, and Dick Lewis grounded out, bringing up Rocky with Wally on deck.

Rocky socked a single through short, but Lee was held up on second by Ken Asher, who was coaching third. Wally, batting fifth today, waited out the pitcher, and got a 2-and-2 count.

He stepped out of the box and dabbed his

hands on the dust to dry the sweat. He took a deep breath and stepped back in. He didn't feel right. He just didn't.

The pitch came in. *Crack!* The ball bounced down to third. The third baseman caught it and stepped on the bag, and the half-inning was over.

The Warriors got a hit in the top of the second, but nothing came of it. When the Pacers came to bat, they rallied for two runs. The Warriors came right back and started pounding Wally without mercy. They got three men on before an out was made.

Coach Hutter called time and walked out to the mound. "Wally," he said, "what's going on out here? If you ever want to be a good pitcher, you've got to learn to concentrate."

"But that's just it, Coach!" Wally blurted. "I don't want to be a pitcher! I just don't feel right in this position."

Coach Hutter looked surprised. After a

moment, he said, "How long have you felt this way, Wally?"

"Always, I guess," Wally said, hanging his head down. "I'm sorry, Coach. I know you hoped I'd be just like Del, but I'm not."

The home plate umpire gave a shout, signaling that time was running out. Either Coach Hutter had to replace Wally or let the game continue. Coach Hutter called for Terry Towns to check in for Wally. Then he walked Wally off the field and sat him down in the dugout.

"Wally, I'm glad you told me how you feel. I'm sorry I put you in such a tough position — and I'm not talking about pitcher, either, though I guess that's been rough on you, too. You and Del were good friends, but that doesn't mean you had the exact same likes and dislikes or strengths and weaknesses. I've just been too blind to see that."

Wally toyed with his glove, then looked up

at the coach. "I miss him, too, Coach," he whispered.

Coach Hutter smiled at Wally, his eyes a warm blue. "Then let's go out there and win this game for him. What do you say?"

Wally breathed deeply. "Does this mean I'm still in the game?"

Coach Hutter smiled at him. "We need your hitting power, fella. You want a chance to get back those runs, don't you?"

Wally's heart leaped. "Yes!" he said happily.

"Okay. Take right field in place of Jamie Ferris. And, Wally —"

"Yes, Coach?"

"When you get to bat, drive that ball down their throats."

Wally's face lit up brightly. "I will!" he cried, and sprinted out to the outfield.

The coach waved Jamie in from right field, talked with Terry a bit on the mound, then walked off the diamond. The crowd cheered for Wally, but the biggest cheer sounded for Terry.

"Come on, Terry!" yelled the fans, as Terry threw in some warm-up pitches. "Let's get those Warriors out!"

Terry pitched hard and did a good job. The Warriors went scoreless for three innings.

Rocky led off again in the bottom of the fifth. He socked a two-one pitch for a double between left and center fields for his third hit of the game. The crowd applauded him. Rocky was having a great day.

Wally stepped to the box. He tapped the tip of his bat upon the hard-rubber plate, then lifted the bat to a spot a few inches over his left shoulder and waited for the pitch.

"Strike!"

Another pitch. He swung. *Crack!*

The ball lifted into the sky toward right field. The crowd started yelling almost immediately. Everyone knew where that ball was going. . . .

Over the fence for a home run!

"Way to go, Wally! That's the way to blast that ball!"

Wally circled the bases. Rocky was waiting for him beside home plate, grinning happily. He shook Wally's hand.

"Beautiful hit, Wally!" he said.

Next, J.J. Adams struck out. Pete Jason walked, then got out on a double play when Jamie hit to short. And the inning was over.

Things popped wide open in the top of the sixth. The first Warrior flied out. But two singles in succession, then a walk, filled the bases. A good hit could put them into the lead again.

In right field Wally tugged nervously on the brim of his cap and bent over, his hands on his knees. Batting for the Warriors was their third hitter in the lineup, a left-hander.

Crack! A high foul fly popped up over home plate.

"I got it!" shouted Chris, throwing his mask aside. "I got it!"

He moved this way and that under the ball. The ball was high — real high. It came plummeting down. Chris put out his mitt.

The ball shot past it, struck the ground. "Oooooo!" groaned the Pacers' fans.

Chris struck the pocket of his mitt angrily and stood there almost a full ten seconds before he gathered up his mask and put it on. He was really disgusted with himself.

Chris returned to his position behind the plate, and Terry stepped to the mound. Terry stretched, delivered.

Smash! A high fly to right field.

Wally ran back, stopped, and waited for the ball. He remembered that a runner was on third. If that runner scored, he would tie up the score. And then, if the man who was now on second got on third, he could be squeezed in and win the ball game for the Warriors.

Wally caught the ball. Without an instant's hesitation he pegged it in to home. The runner was speeding in to score.

The ball struck the ground several feet in front of home plate. It bounced. Chris caught it. He put the ball on the runner who was sliding in to the plate.

Up went the umpire's hand. "Out!" he bawled.

The Pacers' fans leaped to their feet, shouting and screaming with joy. The ball game was over. The Pacers didn't have to take their last raps. They had won 4–3.

The whole team — and some of the fans — crowded around home plate, slapping each other happily on the back.

"A terrific throw, Wally!" cried Coach Hutter. "And a nice put-out, Chris!"

Cab Lacey was there, too. He shook Chris McCray's hand, then Wally's.

"Nice work, both of you," he said. He winked at Wally. He didn't say any more, but Wally knew what he was thinking. *That's the position for you, Wally. In right field. You play best there.*

Some of the players and fans started to drift away.

"Hey, Cab!" Coach Hutter called. "Cab Lacey!"

Cab Lacey turned. With him were Helen, Sharon, and Jeannie.

Coach Hutter walked up to Mr. Lacey. His blue eyes had a glint in them.

"I've just heard some more about you, and it's all good. Sorry about what I said to you last week. I hope you won't hold it against me."

Mr. Lacey grinned. "I have a very poor memory about some things," he said.

"Fine. In that case, how about coaching the team this second half of the season? My job takes me away much of the time anyway. I would certainly appreciate it."

Mr. Lacey shrugged. "Maybe the boys would feel differently about it, Luke."

"Well, let's see about that. What about it, boys?" asked Coach Hutter. "Would you like Mr. Lacey to coach you?"

An enthusiastic shout sprang from them. "Yes, we would!"

Luke Hutter smiled. "There you are. The job's yours."

"Thanks. But I want your help, too," Mr. Lacey said.

"Okay. I'll be your assistant."

The two men laughed over the agreement and shook hands.

"I'm going to add one more thing, Cab," Coach Hutter went on, then paused, as if he didn't quite know how to say what he wanted to. "Well, much as I hate to admit it — since I'm a stubborn mule, as my wife says — Wally does fit better in right field than on the pitcher's mound. That was a nifty peg he made to home. And he seems to hit a lot better when he plays there, too."

He looked at Wally and winked. Coach Hutter was an understanding guy, Wally thought. A real understanding guy.

Wally and Sawbones walked out of the park alongside Cab Lacey and the girls, their parents walking ahead of them. Wally saw Helen making peculiar motions with her fingers to Sharon, and then Sharon making peculiar motions to her.

"Hey!" cried Sawbones. "Look at that sister of yours! She can't talk sign language, can she?"

"You can never tell about *her*," replied Wally. "Sharon, what did Helen say?"

Sharon's eyes twinkled proudly. "She said that you played a wonderful ball game. That you were a hero."

The #1 Sports Writer for Kids

MATT CHRISTOPHER

Read them all!

All available in paperback from Little, Brown and Company

Matt Christopher

Sports Bio Bookshelf

John Elway

Wayne Gretzky

Ken Griffey Jr.

Mia Hamm

Grant Hill

Randy Johnson

Michael Jordan

Lisa Leslie

Tara Lipinski

Mark McGwire

Greg Maddux

Hakeem Olajuwon

Emmitt Smith

Sammy Sosa

Mo Vaughn

Tiger Woods

Steve Young